DIGITAL DIGIMON MONSTERS

WORKING TOGETHER

Adapted by Michael Teitelbaum

based on the Digimon episode
"United We Stand"

by Terri-Lei O'Malley and
Jeff Nimoy & Bob Bucholz

SCHOLASTIC INC.
New York Toronto London Auckland Sydney
Mexico City New Delhi Hong Kong Buenos Aires

Five friends named Davis, Yolei, T.K., and Cody Hida were traveling in the Digital World with their Digimon pals. They stopped near a river to have a picnic.

"Time to eat!" T.K. said. "I am starving."

The Digimon enjoyed a picnic, too.

"Do you have any ketchup?" Gatomon asked.

"I'd like some mustard, please," Hawkmon said.

"These sandwiches are great!"
Dillomon announced.
"I like the chips!" Veemon added.
Patamon just kept on eating.

"There is something I need to talk to you all about," Davis said to his friends. "I would like Ken Ichijoji to join our group. I think he would be a good friend to us all."

"I do not want Ken to join," Yolei replied. "I do not like Ken."

"I do not like Ken, either," Kari said.

"Ken did some bad things,"
T.K. said to the others.
"Some very bad things,"
Cody added. "I do not trust
Ken to be our friend."

"Ken has changed," Davis explained. "He would be a good friend to us now. He and his Digimon companion, Wormmon, would make excellent allies in our battle against evil Digimon. . . ."

"I asked Ken to come and talk with us," Davis continued. "He can show you that he really has changed. I believe we can trust him now. Just give him a chance."

"I guess it is all right to talk with him," Yolei said. "Maybe we should give him a chance to show that he has changed."

An evil creature named Arukenimon appeared suddenly. She had very strong magical powers. "You children always get in my way," she said. "You and your Digimon stop my evil plans. But I will put an end to that right now!"

Arukenimon used her powerful magic to create an evil Digimon named Okuwamon. He was an Ultimate level Digimon, one of the strongest of all Digimon. Okuwamon's Double Scissor Claw attack was very dangerous.

He soared into the air and
roared with all his might.
"Attack them!" Arukenimon
cried, pointing at the five friends.

The evil Digimon landed right in front of the children. He raised his powerful claws to launch his Double Scissor Claw attack.

T.K. turned to his friends. "Our Digimon must act as a team," he announced. "If they work together, they can stop Okuwamon. But first our Digimon must digivolve into more powerful forms!"

Veemon went through an amazing change. He digivolved into ExVeemon. ExVeemon was a very powerful Digimon.

Next, Hawkmon digivolved into powerful Aquilamon.

Then, Dillomon digivolved into Ankylomon.
Now the three Digimon were ready to go!

"I will fire my VeeLaser blast at Okuwamon!" ExVeemon shouted.

But when ExVeemon fired his blast, it bounced right off the evil Digimon.

"I didn't even feel that!" Okuwamon laughed.

"I will try my Blast Rings!" Aquilamon exclaimed.

Aquilamon launched his Blast Rings at Okuwamon. They also bounced off his body.

"Your power is no match for mine!" the evil Digimon shouted.

"My turn!" Ankylomon said.
"Time for my Megaton Press!"
Ankylomon leaped into the air.
He struck with his powerful
Megaton Press. Ankylomon
bounced off the evil Digimon's body.

The evil Digimon moved toward the frightened children. They backed away. "Your attacks were useless!" he shouted. "Now you will feel my power!"

"What can we do now?" Cody cried.

Just then, Ken Ichijoji and Wormmon raced toward the children.

"I am here to help!" Ken shouted.

"Me, too!" Wormmon added.

"Look! It is Ken!" Davis said. "I hope that he and Wormmon can stop the evil Digimon."

"It is hero time, Wormmon!" Ken shouted. Wormmon digivolved into his more powerful form, Stingmon.

Stingmon teamed with the three other good Digimon. He launched his Spiking Strike attack.

Together, working as a team, they defeated the evil Digimon.

After the battle, the children gathered around Ken.
"You were right about Ken," Yolei said to Davis.

"Thank you for helping us, Ken," Kari said. "You are a great part of this team."

"Yes," T.K. agreed. "We would be glad to have you as our friend."

"Thank you for trusting me," Ken replied. "I'm happy to be your friend. I'll never let you down. And neither will my Digimon friend!"